The Jinn

Todd LeRoux

Published by Todd LeRoux, 2024.

This is a work of fiction. Similarities to real people, places, or events are entirely coincidental.

THE JINN

Table of Contents

THE JINN
By
Todd LeRoux

Chapter 1

The last place I wanted to be sanding was on this cliff overlooking the tiny Canadian village of Leading Tickles, a little fishing village sitting on the north-central coast of the island of Newfoundland. The homes of the hard-working fishermen and their families seemed to cling to the very rock of the north Atlantic island. As the night grew around me, I looked up into the stars and wondered how my life had changed so drastically, from the boy I once was, a lad now lost to the tides of time, lost in a world, not of my choosing. The hunter, the killer I have become desperately needing sanctuary.

I find solace in a church most would never have given a second thought of. A small stone building sitting on one of the holiest sites in the new world. There are different sites around the world the sites all hold immense power. Some are very well known, but the most powerful ones are still kept secret. One is in Saskatchewan, Canada; this ancient site holds a large boulder effigy inside a giant stone ring. On the north and south sides of the ring, there are two large stone cairns. The people who built this temple knew it would have to hold a great evil. Another ancient site is located in Germany, though it was destroyed. This site is on the German island of Sylt people now call it a Harhoog. It was a tomb, and for most of the time, this megalithic tomb held great power and could keep evil from the area. Then, mankind, in all our wisdom, ripped it out of its original site and moved it for an airport, destroying its ancient magic. There are other places throughout our world some still remain safe. Most have been destroyed by what I and others of my order have called Jinn. This is a name we took from Arabic; it was the best way to describe the monsters we have fought. Let's start from where I had the misfortune to come into this terrible story.

Before I can tell you about the last two decades of my life, I'll need to inform you of the past, of my family's history. Of how I was to become a pawn in a game. A game where my family would happily sacrifice their only son to keep the wealth and power they covet. My family is an old family. People say our money is old money. That saying only held meaning once I learned about my family's history and how our wealth came to be. This is the history of my damned family; I say damned because if there is a hell, all my ancestors are screaming in its flames.

My family started in the north of France; at the time, the family was not wealthy. At the time, we were so poor my ancestors worked land belonging to another family. My ancestor heard his wife's virtue being called into question by this landlord one day, so this ancestor of mine stood in front of the village square and called the landlord on his lies. To save face, the landlord turned and shot my ancestor. Because the landlord was a great benefactor to the church, he was never brought up on any charges. That night he ordered his men to go to my ancestors' house to kill the wife of my ancestor. This landlord wanted the male child brought to him. The landlord told his men he was going to have the child made into a eunuch. Once this son of my ancestor was healed from his castration, he would be sold in the slave markets of Arabia. Before the landlord's henchmen arrived at my ancestor's home, his wife ran with their infant son. As the wife left the farm, she burned the house and barns to the ground. My ancestor's wife was a gypsy woman; she laid a curse on the land and then disappeared into the night with her son clutched to her chest. She lived and raised her son to hate the landlord and all he stood for. The gypsy wife of my ancestor watched as the son of the man she loved grew. By the time the boy had reached the age of thirteen, he was taller than she remembered his father being. By the time her son was eighteen, he was twice as strong as his father had ever been and so much more handsome.

Men from her family would come by and teach the boy how to fight with his fists, and others taught the boy the art of the sword and axe. Through all this, she watched as her son grew taller and more muscular. They took all the forest could provide and what the rivers gave them. It was a good life. They had a home even though it was a series of caves in a forest no one ventured into, for it was believed to be haunted. The gypsy mother did her best to give her son everything he would need to see him through his life. As the years passed by, the closer she came to her death, the mother knew there was one more thing he would need, that the family would need. Her son watched as his mother aged; the son knew his mother's life would have been easier if it hadn't been for the landlord. The bastard who killed his father the day of his birth, the same man who had sent his henchmen to kill his mother and, as far as he knew to kill him, or worse. If that hateful man had left him and his mother alone, her life would've been easier. The knowledge of how the landlord had never given up on finding his mother to kill. Or him for what the landlord called a life belonging to him as payment for his embarrassment. This caused hatred to grow inside my ancestor. By the time of his twentieth birthday, the hatred had grown and festered inside him to the point where his revenge was all he could think of; it even invaded his dreams. As the years passed, on a warm spring day, the years finally caught up with my ancestor's gypsy mother.

The mother of my ancestor lay on her deathbed. She knew by the rising of the morning sun she would be dead. She remembered when she was a small girl growing up in the hills of Romania. She remembered her grandmother telling her of creatures; they would come to the dying women of their valley. If the dying woman called out the correct incantation and offered what these creatures needed most. One of the creatures would come and grant what the dying wanted most in this world. On the night of her death, by the light of a fading candle, with what strength she had left, the dying mother called out to these creatures and offered what she had left. Laying on her bed, she watched as a shadow shifted. The shadows seemed to roll around, something lurking in a darkened corner of her cave.

The creature seemed to morph from the shadows; its head touched the cave ceiling. The thing looked down on the mother, and something of a smile touched the corners of its mouth.

"I have heard your call, mother. I can do whatever you need of me; however, I will need payment." The creature said as it stood over the dying woman.

"The first part of your payment still beats in my chest; the second part of your payment has yet to come." She replied. Looking down, the Jinn smiled and nodded.

"The first part of the payment seems a little lacking; however, I'm feeling kind this night. About this second part of my payment, what are the terms?" The Jinn asked, smiling.

"The firstborn male child of my sons' bloodline to have this mark will be yours at midnight of his eighteenth year." As she spoke, the dying woman held her hair away from her neck. The creature smiled as the mother revealed a birthmark in the shape of a cross behind her right ear.

"I wish to have every male child who bears this mark to be mine on the night of their eighteenth birthday. It is not so much to ask, not for what I'm about to give your family, is it?" The Jinn looked into her eyes and knew it would get what it wanted.

"No, not so much. You know what I want, you know the payment will be made in the future, so let us be finished. I can feel the light of my life fading; here is the first payment for your services." As she spoke her final words, the old woman held open her robe to the creature standing beside her bed. The Jinn looked at the frail woman, at her shrunken chest. Without saying a word, the Jinn plunged the talons of its right hand into the mother's chest. The creature held her still-beating heart; the Jinn watched as the heart gave its last beat, then nothing. Again the beast smiled as it placed the organ in a golden box it carried.

That is how my ancestor found his mother, her chest splayed open with only her heart missing. The son knew what creature had taken his mother's heart, he knew his mother had called for it, and the son knew his mother had given herself to it. As he buried his mother, the son's anger and hatred grew even more for the landlord. That night the Jinn paid a visit to the son. It explained the deal his mother had made with her. It also explained what would happen if the agreement was ever unfulfilled.

"If ever I do not receive payment, well, then the head of the family will be taken. All the family has gained from our intervention will fall away. The family will return to where it started. Your mother started this for you and your family, so my taking one now and then isn't so bad." When the Jinn finished, she turned and walked into the night. The then young man turned and looked back at the caves where his mother had raised him. Where she had given her very last breath so he could avenge his father and the way the landlord had treated her. He swore a silent vow he would destroy the landlord. My ancestor swore to his dead mother he would wipe the hated landlord's bloodline from the face of the earth.

Chapter 2

The first year after his mother's death, my ancestor found work. He started to save what little wage he earned, then one night, he found a large bag with gold coins in the forest. Knowing if he was caught with the gold, he would be branded a thief and jailed or even hung for having it. He slowly melted it into gold bars and hid them around the forest. As time went on, more and more gold found its way into his stashes. As the year changed seasons, my ancestor watched as his wealth grew. He was surprised by how little time it took to remake himself into a wealthy man from another land. As life would have it, the landlord had been foolish with his money. Now the banks and the crown wanted him to repay some of the debts he owed. Hearing this, my ancestor walked into the bank of the city of Gisors and offered to pay all outstanding debts and tax levies. All he wanted was all titles to the homes and lands in his name. At first, the bank and the crown's representative were skeptical that he had the funds to pay such a large sum. This all changed when he started to unload his saddlebags, and the stack of gold bars grew on the table. Once the gold had been weighed and the tally checked, the crown's representative signed over all lands and houses, with all furniture to my ancestor. Once done, he turned to the local constabulary and told him to inform the former owner of his home he had 24 hours to vacate the house and the land surrounding it. He was to move into a small farm at the far south end of the property, and he could use it rent-free until he passed on.

When word of what had transpired at the bank and the crown had excepted full payment of his debts from a stranger. Effectively making the former landlord poor and bankrupt. The former landlord was being given a chance to live on the farm. It was the same farm he was forced to rebuild after he killed the man who dared to call him a liar and farmed for him. He sent men to get the farmer's wife, to kill her, and bring the whelp of the farmer to him. The gypsy woman ran into the night; no matter what he did, no one could ever find the gypsy woman. She burnt the barns and the house to the ground. There were places where you could grow enough to keep a small family alive. Now his fate and that of his daughter rested there, the former landlord could only hope his family connections with the crown would get him out of this mess, and he will regain his lands and title before long. Standing on the front step of what was once his manner house, the former landlord watched as a big young man, on the finest Friesian stud he ever laid eyes on, cantered up to him. Watching as the young man stepped from the saddle to the ground, the former landlord knew he would never be a match for the young man in a duel.

My ancestor looked at the man who had killed his father and then chased his mother into the wild with a newborn. He wanted to march up to the man and kill him on the steps of the house he had built on the backs of others.

"The farm I let you live on, you should be able to feed yourself and your family. Remember, these lands and the other houses are no longer yours, be so kind as to remove yourself from them." Without another word, he brushed past the former landlord, walked into his house, and shut the door without looking back. The now-seething former owner of the house looked at the beautiful Friesian stud. He wanted to walk to the horse, cut its throat with his dagger then be on his way. The man knew his life would be forfeit if he touched the animal. The former landlord watched as the door to what was once his home opened, and his daughter walked down the stairs. She smiled at him, and he knew of all the things he had done in his life; being her father was the best of all of them. He smiled back, took her hand, and walked away from his home.

The years passed, and my ancestor would ride down to the small farm and watch the landlord and his daughter as they worked the land. The servants at the main house would come and tell him if the man and his daughter had a good year. They would see her in town selling wool or extra milk. Their flock of sheep had grown, and now they produced more wool than any other farm in the area. My ancestor watched the former owner of the land and his daughter fight to make a living on the small farm. His hatred only grew as the years passed. Then one day, the old butler told my ancestor, the former landlord and owner of the house, was on death's door. He said most people didn't think the old man would make it through the night. That night my ancestor rode to the small farm. Stopping at the gate, he stepped from the saddle, knowing what he was going to do, a smile playing at the corners of his lips. Looking around to ensure he wasn't being watched, he knocked on the door of the tiny house. The farmer's beautiful daughter answered when she saw who it was at their door; she stepped back and let him enter.

"What sees you to this door tonight?" She asked. The daughter never hid the fact she hated him for what she considered an injustice to her father.

"I have heard your father is not well. I have come to tell him a secret and see him into the next life." My ancestor smiled at the daughter. Being a good daughter, she showed him into the room where the now dying old man lay. When the faded eyes of the former landlord looked up, they knew who had come to the door of his home. He hated my ancestor for being able to see him so weak.

"What is it you want now? Is it not enough you have taken all my lands and homes? Now you want to take my peaceful death too?" He asked in a horsed whisper.

"No, I don't want your peaceful death. I came to tell you a secret. One I have kept from you all these years now. A man and wife once lived on this land and worked it for you. You saw fit to go around town and soil the man's wife with your lies. When the man called you a liar, you shot him in the back. That night you sent your henchmen to kill the wife of this farmer to bring their baby boy to you. You planned to have the baby castrated and sold into slavery in the land of the moors." After my ancestor recounted all that happened in the past. The former landlord looked closely at the man that stood at the foot of his deathbed.

"How, how is it you...?" The dying man started to ask.

"The man you killed was my father, the woman who ran into the night with a newborn baby in her arms and the blood of my birth still warm on her legs was my mother."

"You, you have taken everything from me; if your father had known his place, he would be alive today. I owned all this, and he called me a liar, all over some gypsy whore." The old man wanted to goad my ancestor into pulling his pistol and shooting him. This way, his daughter could go to the crown and sue for the return of the lands and houses. Instead, what happened next the old man didn't see coming.

"Well, I haven't taken all from you, not yet, old man." Just as he finished the sentence, the daughter walked into the room. Turning, my ancestor looked at the beautiful young woman, pulled his belt knife, and ran the razor-sharp blade across her throat. It was so fast the daughter felt the warmth of her blood as it spilled down the front of her dress. Her last sight was of her blood splashing across her father's face before the weakness came over her, and she fell across the dying man's legs.

"You, you..." The old man stuttered as he looked down on his dead daughter.

"Yes, I know you old fuck, I killed her. Now you will learn the price of your actions toward my mother." My ancestor hissed at the dying man.

"I did that; my daughter was innocent. She was but a babe when I wronged your mother." The old man said as he stroked his dead daughter's hair.

"As was I; you thought you had the right to own my life, to sell into slavery. Well, when I leave this place, I'm going to have your useless son gelded and then sold as you would have me."

"Then kill me, you monster and be done with it." The old landlord said as he stared at my ancestor.

"Killing you outright would be a kindness. This is something I'm not willing to offer you. My mother burnt this place to the ground once. I think it is only fitting for it to be raised to the ground once more." As the story goes, my ancestor threw an oil lamp into the corner of the room. Then he walked out of the tiny house, the dying screams of the old man following him into the night. My ancestor sat on the top of the hill to the north of the farm, smiling as he watched the burning thatch roof cave in. The cows and sheep scattered into the mountains and fields. My ancestor let the horses out of the barn before he had set that ablaze. He knew they would find their way to the main house and barns. With a final look, he turned and rode back to his home and a job with the old man's son.

Chapter 3

As time went on, my ancestor became known as a lord. His wealth and power brought him to the homes of the most powerful in France. During one of these parties, he met his future wife and the mother of his four sons. Life went on for my ancestor and the family, sons came, and war took a few. As promised, the firstborn with the mark was given to the Jinn at midnight on his eighteenth birthday. This started a tradition in my family, and it was a sad thing. When a boy child was born, if he had the mark, the family would consider him dead at birth. The only reason he was given everything he wished for was that the family knew he would be a burden for a short time. Most other families the Jinn have helped have had, at some point in time, stopped the gifts of their first sons. Because of this, they have lost their wealth, and my family will do anything to keep their wealth and power. The cost of one of their children was of no matter to them. Hell, I can remember my mother saying if her children were to die, she could just buy two or three more. She said she would get them in any colour to match any outfit. That's the kind of family I had the misfortune to be born into; lucky me. So this is where I begin trying to find out what the hell the Jinn are and where they come from. How the hell do I kill them and simultaneously fuck my mother and father over just because they deserve it.

It's funny; my father sent me to a school in the south of France. He told me being away from family builds a strong man, one not given to emotion. So I went to school. In the twelve years I spent in school, I have only been home for a holiday twice. Most of the other time, I spent in the library or roaming the halls of the school. Some of the time, I could be found in the forests that hold the foot of the mountains and valleys in their shadows. I would get a call once and a while from my mother, usually when she felt guilty for dumping her firstborn in a school. For the last two years, I had started hanging up the phone before any words were spoken. My action toward my mother angered my father. He called the school's headmaster, demanding I talk to my mother when she called. I was given a talking to about my responsibility to my family, and he told me it is never easy for a mother to leave a child. He was shocked when I told him for her, it was a piece of cake to leave me behind and that I held no love for my family.

"Sir, this might sound cold and hard-hearted, but I do not wish to ever hear that woman's voice again," I said. I looked my headmaster in the eye. To his credit, he just nodded and leaned back in his chair.

"Well, who can blame you, really? You've been here with me for twelve years, and in that time, I can only remember you going away two times, maybe. I can not sit here and lecture you on how to act toward them." When Mr. Normandeau finished what he wanted to say, he simply shuffled some papers on his desk. It was his way of saying I could leave. Still furious that my father would call the school to complain about how his wife was being treated by their son. The son, whom they've not seen fit to visit for four years, was burning me up when Lisa, one of my oldest and best friends, grabbed my arm. She could tell I was upset; she let go of my arm and walked beside me for a while. Lisa was a good person and a great friend; she and Jack were my only real friends here. They were the only ones who knew what my family was like. Well, not the whole sacrifice of your firstborn son so he can have his heart cut out, hell I didn't even know that at this point. They just knew about how I was dumped here and forgot about it. Lisa was sent here to protect her from her father's competitors. His company was the world's largest computer and software firm. From the day she was born, her mother and father have had to keep her under a blanket of security. Only at this school can Lisa move around without her armed guards; then there's Jack, the best-kept secret in the world.

No, I kid you not; he is the son of JFK Jr, let that sink in for a second, the grandson of John F Kennedy. His family hid Jack here to keep him safe from the assassins who killed his grandfather, granduncle, and father. Even these two hunted and hounded friends of mine get to go home for holidays. Their families always offer to have me spend time with them, but I refuse, knowing it would anger my father. I don't care if he gets angry with me. I worry about what he would do if he thought one of the families was trying to embarrass him or the family. So I sit alone, and the hatred for my father and mother grows. Here of late, the woman who gave birth to me has tried to call me on several different days of the week. First, I thought her guilt about abandoning her firstborn must be getting to her, and she needed to appease her guilt. Then my father called for the first time in two years. I decided to talk to him, but the call was short and to the point. He told me when my mother called, I was to pick up the phone on the first ring, and I was to be nice to her. It was at that point in the conversation I informed my father he could go fuck himself and hung up. If I'm going, to be honest with you, that wasn't the smartest thing I could have done. Lisa had overheard my end of the conversation. She wasn't eavesdropping. I was shouting in rage, and her room and mine share a wall, so being the great friend she is, she and Jack knocked on my door, then walked in and sat to listen to me vent about my fucked up family. This was a month before my eighteenth birthday, and what I now know should have been my last birthday. This is the story of a fight to survive monsters, the rip-your-heart-out kind of monsters. They fight to survive different kinds of monsters, my family's kind of monsters.

Chapter 4

My birthday falls on the start of summer, June 21; it turns out I was an afternoon baby, as it also turns out. June 21 is the day after I would have graduated from school, then headed off to university with Lisa and Jack. However, a month before graduation, I started to see strange people lurking in the forests surrounding the school. At first, I was worried for my friends, knowing how many threats surrounded them each day. Every time I tried to show one of the others the strangers, it was as if they would vanish like mist over a lake. One night I came awake, convinced someone was watching me through my dorm window. I could remember a fleeting image of a pair of yellow eyes. After that night, I started to bolt my window and draw the curtains. I began to check and recheck my room every night and check the halls outside my door. A week before graduation, my mother tried to call me six times. I decided to answer the phone the sixth time. Though I never really liked my mother, I was shocked to hear her rage at the phone, not knowing I had answered.

What I heard ended what little liking I had held out for my family. I heard her tell my father it would be cause for celebration the night the beasts take my heart. My mother told my father she wished they could be there to see it happen. She ranted about how I was nothing more than an expense the family didn't need. I thought about calling back to scream at her about being an inhuman bitch, then thought about it. I knew I didn't need my family or their money. Over the years, my father has sent me a fortune. I thought it was to ease his guilt, but then hearing what I had over the phone, I knew it was a payment for services rendered. Looking around my dorm room, I knew I wouldn't miss anything here; it was all throwaway stuff. What I needed most, what I couldn't do long without, were Lisa and Jack and as if right on cue, Lisa knocked on my door.

"I take it you heard the big bang, huh?" I asked as she swung the door open.

"Oh yeah, what the hell happened?" Jack asked as he came in behind Lisa.

"Well, it seems I've been nothing but a burden to my family, a mistake. I got that from the crazy bitch, when she had forgotten to hang up the phone. She didn't realize I had picked up and could hear every word she said." I told my friends.

"Bitch." Both my friends said at the same time.

"So now, I need to find a bank where I can hide my money, one my father has nothing to do with," I told them as I stood up, looking out my dorm room window. I had a terrible feeling of being watched from the treeline. The creature kept to the shadows, staying far enough in the forest so the afternoon sunlight couldn't lay on its skin.

"If you want, I could ask my father if he could help and maybe move your money for you," Lisa said as she walked over to me.

"No...no, I can't get either of your families involved in this; I know my mother and father. I know what they will try and do if they ever found out I received help from your families."

"Well, this is complete bullshit, pal," Jack stated.

"I know, for some reason, I think if I can get away and hide out for a year or two, I think I'll be safe," I said, turning away from the window.

"You're not going to leave before graduation, are you?" Lisa asked as she turned to look to Jack for help if I said that I was.

"No, I'm going to stick around for that; it would seem suspicions if I up and disappeared," I said.

In hindsight, I should have taken off that night or the following day; I was naive. So I spent my time between the school and the bank in the small town that housed the school. Though it was a small town in the southwestern part of France. It boasted some of the best personal security on the planet. My father never took my safety for granted. I had a team of men he had hired away from the United States secret service for my bodyguards. When I wished to go into town, they would be with me every step of the way, hell I couldn't even go to the bathroom alone. Looking back on that time in my life, I now know the security my mother and father had for me wasn't for my safety. It was to keep my heart and virtue intact until it could be harvested. The school my friends and I attended was in the small town of Gedre; I loved this part of France. The town was in the Parc National Des Pyrenees at the foot of the mountain Massif Du Neouville. Being such a small place, I would have difficulty coming and going without being noticed. I had to do everything with my security team hovering over me the whole time.

Chapter 5

On my first trip into town, I went shopping for what I thought I would need to get me through the mountains, a backpack, sleeping bag, good hiking boots, warm clothing, and assorted goods and foods that were light to carry. Some of my security team became curious about some of my purchases.

"You planning to go someplace we should know about Rod? John, the head of my security, asked me on the ride back to school.

"Well, after graduation Lisa and Jack and I plan to do some hiking through the mountains, you know to see if we can find some ruins of the Greeks or Phoenicians who first settled this region of modern France," I answered, I knew when I would start spouting history or other obscure facts about France, most of my team would shut me out and resort to their internal monologue.

"Just let me know so I can have it checked out first, ok," John said. It wasn't a request, so I nodded and turned to watch the forest pass by my window. The second and third trips into town were to the bank to transfer funds into another bank. This bank is on a small, very wealthy island in the south pacific. The monarch who rules this island is no dumb native. He was educated in England and the US, knows their tax laws, and has opened his island to the wealthiest men and women in the world. It took some doing, but I finally reached the ruler and head banker of this island and explained everything to him. I used his extreme dislike for my father to win him over, though he wouldn't answer me over the phone on our first meeting. The monarch told me he would be in contact with me in a week. Good to his word, the call I was waiting for came in. I almost jumped for joy when he told me he would accept my money and personally invest it.

"Sir, you have made my starting a new life easier. Thank you so much," I said.

"No son should have to live away from his family as you have. The next communication we have will be through one of my people in your area, good luck Rod." I didn't trust my father or mother, so I had Lisa buy me a burner cell phone on one of her trips into town; I used this burner phone to do all my banking. By graduation, I was ready to start my run for freedom, which I should have started a month sooner.

Standing at the podium overlooking my classmates and their families. I could see strange people sifting through the crowds. I finished my speech, turning. I left the stage, ducked behind it, then ran for the dorm building as fast as I could. I was going to make my run starting after the grad celebrations. I was ready; everything was packed. Throwing my robes off as I ran down the hallway, I could hear someone running behind me. As I turned down the hall where my room was, I looked back to see a tall woman chasing me. She was smiling at me. I could see the door to my room, and I ran past the entrance to Jack's room. The night before, Lisa talked me into placing my backpack in Jack's room and all my banking paperwork. At the time, I thought she was just making sure I didn't leave before our graduation. I grabbed my things as fast as I could, then opened the window, starting my escape. I had just let go of the window sill when I heard Jack's door crash open.

As I ran for the area where the cars were parked, I turned to see the woman chasing me standing at the window with another man; she wasn't smiling. I had wanted to steal the SUV my security team used to take me to town. Jack said it would have a GPS unit, allowing my team to find me. So I decided to take Mr. Crags' car, all the students and I laughed at his vehicle. It was an older citron, but it was reliable, and he never took the keys out of the ignition. Before I knew it, I was driving through the school gates. I sped onto the road, making me a car thief. Four miles out of town, I made my first major decision. The road split 921 headed south, and the other 922 headed deeper into the mountains. Before I knew why I was rolling down the 922, heading deeper into the mountains. I had a new burner phone showing me the way using google maps. I drove off into the night. I could have made better time by driving faster than the posted speed limit. I didn't want to deal with the police. I didn't think the little citron could outrun a cop car.

I knew my security team had updated my father; they were hunting me down by this time. Getting pulled over by the police was the last thing I needed. I knew where I was going, and I also knew this road ended at a parking lot for people who wanted to explore that part of the Pyrenees mountains. From that parking area, it was only fifty-five miles into Spain, it was going to be a challenging climb, but I knew I could do it. So with my sights set on getting over the mountains into Spain, I followed the twin beams of light from the citron into the night.

The moon was high in the sky when I reached the end of the road. As I parked the car, I realized how large my task was ahead of me. I knew if I stood there too long, I would talk myself out of my plan and that indecision would cost me time, which in my case, would mean my life. I knew by now the people who called themselves my mother and father were frantic. They weren't worried I would be hurt in the mountains. They were worried I would fall and kill me, thus breaking the contract the old gypsy mother had begged for all those years past. They both knew if I died, my father's heart would take my place, and the family would lose everything.

I could imagine how the conversation went when John called to tell my mother and father I had gone missing, and from what they could tell, I had stolen a car to make good my escape. I was young then, well, younger anyway. I never thought about the wildlife that could do me harm as I jogged into the mountains holding the border between France and Spain in them.

I knew I wanted to get to Barcelona from there. I could go anywhere in the world if I could book a passage on a ship. The first night I kept moving the whole night. I never realized I had climbed two passes and was in the valley of my third when the sun started to light the peaks of the mountains. On my second day, I slept under an overhang; it was cool in the shade. I had a stream fed by the snow melt to replenish my water. As I woke, I could hear others nearby; they sounded German. I stayed hidden under my overhang, not wanting anyone to see me. For three days, I climbed by the light of the moon and slept under cliffs or boulders. Early into the fourth day of my run for freedom, I walked out of the mountains onto a road. I knew I was in Spain when I came to the first sign for the nearest town. I desperately wanted a hot shower and a soft bed. I didn't want to stop yet, so I found a cafe open all night and asked for a bus stop.

Chapter 6

Lisa was a lot craftier than either Jack or I gave her credit for. Her security detail stood by as John asked her if she or Jack knew I was going to run away. Lisa looked at him and told John she was mad at me for leaving before our prom; she acted like the spoiled rich kid the team expected. When they realized she wouldn't be of any help, they headed out. By this time, they knew what car to look for, and they surmised I would be trying to get into Spain. It never occurred to my security or family that I would hike over the mountains into Spain. They alerted the Spanish emigration and customs to watch for me. So three and a half days later, I walked over the border and, at the first town, bought a bus ticket to Barcelona; no one was the wiser. It took me a total of five days to reach Barcelona. It took me another two to find a ship's Captain willing to take a young man anywhere the ship was going. When the Captain of the tramp freighter asked why I was out in the world, I told the truth. I had just graduated and wanted to see the world before my young life ended. When the Captain became concerned and asked if I was ill, I smiled and told him it was a figure of speech.

"It's my way of saying before my father makes me join the family business," I told the Captain.

"Well, it's good for a young man to see the world, to know how things work out there." He said as he waved his arm toward the ocean. So my real education started, I was a paying passenger, and as such, I wasn't expected to work. I would lend a hand on the deck once in a while. Mostly I helped with securing the sea containers and if some ropes needed to be tidied up, stuff like that. It kept me busy, and the deckhands seemed to like me helping. It had taken a few days for the crew to warm up to the rich kid on their ship. I would sit and listen to the men talk to each other as the ship rode the endless waves. One of the men found me doing push-ups on deck one day. He asked if I wanted to work out with him and two of his friends. That night I started learning jujitsu; the three men on the ship were great teachers. They taught me every night, and the Captain began sitting in on our sessions. The trip across the Mediterranean was excellent; the seas were calm, and the winds were fair. So before I knew it, the port of Said was gliding past us on our way to the Suez canal. The Captain explained we would travel through the canal and eventually reach the Arabian sea. Then from there, we were bound for Japan.

"It will take us a month or so to reach our destination." The Captain told me as we stood at the deck railing. I knew my father was searching the world for me. As I stood at the railing with the Captain, I started to worry I may have gotten the man in trouble he didn't need. I wondered how far my security team had gotten as we exited the canal. Did they find my trail into the mountains? If so, do they know I went to Barcelona and boarded this ship? I then thought about the woman and the others who had been around the school before I had taken off. I knew they had something to do with my family. I just couldn't think it through for now.

My family's team had found where I had left the car. John, my security team leader, tried to tell my father he thought I would be hiking in the mountains. My father being the man he is, said he would never be caught hiking. My father's ego wouldn't let him think his son could or would do something he couldn't. So after John informed my father he didn't know me as well as he thought, my father fired him. When Lisa heard John was fired, she hurriedly called her father and asked if she could have John as her security team leader.

It took over a month for our ship to reach Japan. I stood on the ship's deck, thanking the Captain and crew for allowing me to travel with them. I turned and walked down the gangway and out of the port. I found a cab and asked the driver to take me to a youth hostel if he knew of one. The driver dropped me off at the hostel. When he did, I stood astounded by the city of Tokyo.

Chapter 7

I knew I would need help trying to stay ahead of my family. I still wanted to keep in touch with Lisa and Jack; however, I couldn't put them at risk. In my young mind, I thought I could find a place where I could learn to fight. I knew I had the money to pay for my time here as long as I stayed out of businesses wanting a credit card. I found a youth hostel for young travellers and booked a room for a week; I paid cash up front and started to explore the Shinto shrines in and around Tokyo after a week of trying to find a place where they would still teach a young man how to protect himself in secret. I was about to give up when an old man, whose back had bent from years of hard labour, took my arm and smiled at me. He led me to a table where he sat and waited for me to pour him a small cup of tea.

"You ask many questions, and someone listens. They have agreed to teach you. This being said, you can not stay here in this city." The old man told me as he sipped his tea, then handed me a piece of paper. I watched as he stood and shuffled off into the mass of humanity moving through Tokyo. Sitting with my small cup of tea still in my hand, I look at the piece of paper I was handed. I looked around to see if anyone had taken any interest in the old man or me. As far as I could tell, everyone had gone about his or her day. That day I returned to the hostel and packed my belongings. The note I was handed told me to book a ticket to the island of Shikotan. The paper held the name of this island and the name of a man I was to ask for when I stepped off the ferry. I could read the note; it was written in neat English. The name, on the other hand, was in traditional Japanese calligraphy. It was beautiful to look at, but as for reading it well, I was utterly at a loss.

As I walked to the train station, I felt I was just ahead of my father and mother, along with the others who had been at my school. My birthday had come and passed if I had known I had placed my family, especially my father, in harm's way, it wouldn't have made a difference to me. At this point, I realized I had no use for my family. To tell the truth, the only ones I recognized as my family were just leaving school in France to go home. Jack and Lisa were indeed my only family. While I was away from them, I craved to hear Jack's laugh and Lisa's voice telling me everything was going to be alright.

Sitting on the train, I watched as the landscape of Honshu, the largest of the Japanese islands, blurred past my window. Before I left Tokyo, I bought five more disposable cell phones. I knew in the Japanese culture, it was bad manners to talk loudly on a phone while others were around. It was the ultimate insult to those around you if you had your phone on speaker while taking a call. Knowing this, I looked around at the other passengers and then found a quiet spot out of the way where I could call Lisa.

"Where are you, no wait, do tell me, are you safe?" Lisa asked before I could even tell her who was calling.

"I'm safe, and how did you know who was calling? I've changed phones. How are Jack and the others?" I asked her, trying to keep up on the news, especially when it came to what my mother and father would be doing anything trying to find me.

"Well, your mother and father came to the school and had a special security team go through your room. They wanted to search my room and Jack's. My father was here and put a stop to it; I thought it would come to blows at one point. That's when John, my new head of security, stepped in and informed your father he had no rights nor the authority to search anything other than your room. I thought he was going to explode, then his security team leader eased your father back, and they stormed off." Lisa told me.

"I was wondering how far they got on my trail or if they know how I made out of Spain?" I asked, hoping she would know.

"Hang on, Jack wants to talk to you," Lisa said.

"Hey brother, about how far they've gotten, well, they know that you crossed into Spain over the mountains, very cool, I might add very cool, and they found where you bought a bus ticket. After that, they've come up with a big fat nothing; they say it's as if you've dropped off the world." When Jack finished his news, I could hear Lisa telling him to give her the phone back. Listening to the two of them banter back and forth brought a smile to my face. I had been without my friends for so long that the smile felt foreign. At the same time, I could feel the tears start to burn my eyes. God damn, my mother and father, this was supposed to be the best part of my life, not the part where I'm trying to survive on my own.

"Listen, Rod, Jack and I are going home tomorrow, don't call from this phone again. Do you remember the first year we came to this school?" Lisa asked; it had been twelve years ago.

"Yes, I remember. What of it?" I asked.

"Do you remember our first mathematics teacher? Do you remember our first *mathematic* teacher?" She asked; in our first year, we didn't take mathematics. I was about to remind Lisa we didn't take that course in our first year when she said she and Jack loved me and hung up, leaving me to listen to the buzz of a deadline. Looking at my phone, I thought about the word mathematics, then it hit me. It was like a cypher. At least, I thought it was a code, so I sat down and wrote the alphabet down, then matched each letter with a number. When I was finished, I had a phone number, 1-312-085-1312 extension 9319. Looking at the number, I wondered if I should call it now or wait. Before I could stop myself, I dialled the number and sat listening to it ring on the other end.

"Rod, I'm glad you called." Lisa's father said as he answered.

"Now, this is going to be short; you just need to listen, ok?"

"Yes, sir," I answered.

"If you can find your way to a small island in the Japanese archipelago, this island is called Shikotan. I have a very special old friend who lives there. He will teach a young man in your situation all he needs to know. My friend or another from his temple will be waiting for you. Hurry, and after this call, this number will be out of service; good luck, son." Lisa's father said as he ended the call. I was going to tell Lisa's father I was already in Japan, but I never had the chance. As soon as he was finished wishing me luck, the man I greatly respected ended the call. As I was on a train heading to the island of Shikotan, I thought I was finally having good luck. Again I turned and watched as the island of Honshu raced past the train window. Hours later, it felt odd when I was standing on the platform after the blurring speed of the bullet train ride. Now I and some other passengers stood on another platform, all of us waiting for a bus to take us to the ferry terminal. Looking around, I watched the other people on the platform. None of them seemed to be interested in me, then, with a hiss of air breaks, our bus stopped. I climbed on the bus and sat in the last seat. As I sat in the back seat of the bus, I again looked at the people who had stepped off the train with me.

The bus driver kept looking in his mirror at me, and for the first couple of times, I wondered if I should be worried. Then it came to me. I was a tall white boy. Some would say I was a ginger. Looking up at the bus driver, I nodded and smiled, hoping this small gesture would put the man at ease. I sighed with relief when the older man smiled, gave a slight nod in return, and concentrated on the road ahead.

The ferry terminal came into sight as the bus rounded another in the endless turns through the villages of this part of Japan. Standing, I walked to the front of the bus to leave when the driver reached out and touched my arm.

"You must be careful; some are about." He whispered, then looked out his window. Stepping off the bus, I looked around and walked with my fellow passengers to get our tickets. The sun was brighter as I stood in line to board the ferry that would take me to the island of Shikotan. With Lisa's father's warning and then the bus driver, I can say I was on guard for anything. Looking around, I felt uneasy about the ferry ride to the small island. A petite elderly lady came by and looked at the seat I occupied; smiling, I stood offering her my seat. A man sitting behind me looked annoyed that I had moved; I decided some fresh air would be nice. Walking on the deck, I could watch for the man; I wanted to see if he followed me out or was just having a bad day. I never saw the man until we docked and were starting to leave the ferry. I saw the annoyed man again. This time he was talking to another, and they both turned and looked at me; it was then I knew I had been found.

Just when I was about to run, a small cool hand clasped mine; in shock, I looked down to see the old lady holding my hand; she was smiling up at me. Not knowing what to do, I smiled back, then let her lead us off the ferry. The two men watched and looked at their phones; I was starting to get nervous; I think the old lady could feel this. She pulled me to a stop, and in a voice more assertive than I could have thought possible for a person her size, she told me.

"Do not let them see your fear. It's what they want; if you run now, they know they have you. Just walk with me; we are safe. Your friends have made sure we will make it home." When she finished talking, I looked over my shoulder and saw one of the men falling in step behind us. I did my best to let him know he didn't bother me, and that's when I saw his eyes for the first time. His eyes were yellow, and the pupil was oval like a cat's. For the first time, I could see what they showed the rest of the world was nothing more than a cover-up. A mask trying to hide what he really was. To this day, I don't know what came over me. Before I could stop myself, I winked at the creature following the old lady and me. My lack of fear infuriated the beast. It let out a sound caught between a low growl and a hiss. Turning, I could see the second thing from the ferry standing in the middle of a crowd. This one was trying to block our path; I smiled and then turned to the older lady.

"Ma'am, these things are here for me, and I don't want you to be hurt. You must leave me; I'll be alright," I said as I tried to take my hand back.

"Oh, I know they are here for you, so am I, and I found you first, so they are going to have to wait. Now come with me." She said as she pulled me into a shop. A young woman working behind the counter smiled at us. The young shop lady moved to close the door when the creature followed the old lady, and I tried to force its way in. Turning, I watched as the girl pulled a sword from an umbrella rack and drove it into the creature's chest. Dark purple blood ran from the wound as it staggered back, seeming surprised to see the colour of its blood. I looked down at the weathered smiling face of the kind old lady. The bravery I saw in her eyes bolstered my courage. After all, how could I be afraid when I had when this older lady who showed so much courage?

"Who was she?" I asked as we exited the shop through the back door and then moved into a crowd shopping at a market.

"She sees the truth; we know how most of the richest families in the world have come to be." My guide answered as she led the way through the crowds. Before I realized where I was, my guide and I had left the shops and the public, and we entered a forest. As I turned, I could see the creature who had been stabbed being helped by the second one standing at the edge of the woods. For some reason, they wouldn't or couldn't enter the forest, so being myself, I turned and raised my hand, waving to them. I looked at my guide. She was mimicking me and was also waving.

"Now come, we are almost home; here, you will learn all you need to know to survive your curse." My guide said as she retook my hand.

Chapter 9

The path through the forest I found myself being led through on the small island of Shikotan ended at the gates of an ancient temple. I could see a small group of men standing waiting for us; the old lady looked up at me and smiled.

"This is going to be your home for quite a while. It will give you sanctuary. These men will teach you the art of defeating the Jinn; here is where your family can not get at you." When my guide finished telling me I would be safe, I looked back to the men waiting for us. I came to a stop when a man who I recognized stepped out from behind the others. He smiled at my recognition and stepped forward to hug me.

"My boy, am I glad you made it. I know you have many questions, so for now, let's get inside and talk." He said as I was surrounded and ushered into a building.

"How, why are you here, sir? Is Lisa ok?" I started to ask when he smiled.

"Lisa and Jack are fine. I'm here because this is where I came to train as a young man like yourself. Rod, this is going to be hard to hear. I think you already know. Deep down, you know something is wrong with your family." Lisa's father said.

"Yes, I guess I have known for some time my mother and father are not, well, normal. I always felt as if I was being held out for the slaughter, as it were. The things I was to be delivered to came to the school, waiting to collect their prize, the night I made a run for it. I'm guessing I threw the proverbial monkey wrench into their plans." I told the group sitting around the table.

"How did you know to run? As far as you could've known, they could have been another security team sent in by your father?" One of the men asked as he poured tea into a small cup.

"I didn't know who they were; I could tell they wanted me. At the start of my senior year, I started planning my run just to be free of my family. Then the day I took off, a woman chased me into the dorm building of my school. She moved, unlike anyone I ever saw before."

"So you ran, then when you couldn't drive anymore you hiked through the mountains to Spain?" Lisa's father asked as he sipped his tea.

"Yes sir, then once I made it into Spain, I bought a bus ticket to Barcelona; that's where I found passage on a freighter to Tokyo." I finished.

Lisa's father turned to the others and smiled.

"Well, he's braver than I was when I came to you, and I might add he can see them for what they are." When Mr. Graves finished, he picked up his cup of tea and smiled at me. I watched as the oldest among them stood and walked over to me. I didn't feel right sitting as this man walked to me, so I stood.

"My sister tells me you turned and winked at one of the beasts as he was following you. She tells me you can see under the masks they wear. You can see their eyes." Without realizing it, I had gotten down on one knee while this elderly man looked into my eyes.

"Yes, sir, I can; they have eyes like a cat; they are yellow with a vertical pupil," I told him. I watched as he nodded, patted my head, and turned.

"You are home now, son; you will stay here until you are ready to go out into the world and fight these things. Maybe soon we will rid the world of this evil." I was told.

"Rod, you are going to become part of a vast family, I was brought here when I was young by my father. He refused to have his son killed for nothing more than money. These Jinns killed him. I rebuilt my family fortune and have been hunting Jinn my whole adult life. I have talked to Lisa, and she now knows what's at stake here."

"Well, if you've told your daughter, then it's a safe bet she's let Jack in on what's going on," I added as he nodded his head.

"But sir, if the Jinn knows where I am, won't they come for me sooner rather than later?" I asked as others started to enter the room.

"Well, there are certain places on the earth these creatures can't set foot on; we don't understand why. Many decades ago, your new family had a Jinn prisoner. After time this prisoner gave up some secrets. It told the elders at the time of places safe from his kind. It has to do with some kind of crystal formation and the frequency they vibrate at. This is one of those places you will learn of the others, on each of these places, we have a temple. These temples have been on these spots for hundreds of years." As Lisa's father finished, I saw my two best friends in the world and the only family I had ever known escorted into the room. Before I could stop myself, I ran to Lisa and Jack. The three of us stood hugging in the middle of the group; John, my former head of security, smiled at me.

"Good to see you, Rod. Hiking over the mountains was taking a chance; it threw us off just long enough; I'm glad you made it. Now that I know the truth, I'll be staying with you." John told me as he placed a hand on my shoulder. I felt safer with him standing in the room with me.

"I'm staying too, my father has told me about these things your family wanted to give you, and well, I want to end their power hold on the world," Lisa said as she stood on the other side of John.

"Well, hell, you didn't think I would let you guys go off on this grand adventure without me, did you?" Jack asked as he joined Lisa.

"I didn't want you guys to be in danger; that's why I left the way I did," I told the others as I stepped toward Lisa's dad.

"I know my family only thinks of me as a burden they had to pay for until the day of my eighteenth birthday. Then they would be rid of me, and they get to keep all they love. To me, you guys are my real family; I never want to see anything hurt you." I said as Lisa started to wipe her tears away.

"God damn it, Rod, now look, you've made me cry." Lisa started to say as Jack handed her a hankie.

"And about that young man." Another younger version of the old lady spoke out.

"You do realize your father must pay for your decision to come here. Your father will forfeit his life, and your family will lose all it has gained over the years. Can you live with that?" She asked as she stepped closer to me.

"If they were anybody else, if they had have used what they had gained for the betterment of mankind. Then yes, I could see myself hating myself for this action. However, you need to know the kind of people who call themselves my parents. They delight in the destruction of others, and they get a sense of power from hurting others. Whole families have fallen to them, and they laugh, and as for the man who donated his sperm to the egg donor, no, I won't feel anything for them." I told the whole room. I could hear Lisa giggle and John shuffling his feet. The lady who asked me the question turned and nodded to another in the room. This man was holding a large book in front of his chest, and I watched as he stepped forward.

"Now that you have entered our ranks, you will learn all you need to know to kill the Jinn. This will be your first lesson, including you." The man told us, including John.

"Sir, I'm only here to make sure the kids are safe," John told the smiling man.

"What better way to make sure they are safe? You must train with them and learn what it is they seek to accomplish." I watched as the man placed the book into John's hands. When he looked from the book to Lisa's dad, he started to smile.

"Alright, it looks like we are going to be classmates." Our protector said as he held the book. Lisa's father took her by the hand and led her to another room. I knew he was telling her something we would need to know in the future. As it turned out, it was the one piece of information that would save us all in times to come, just not in time. The following day our new lives started. It was a shock to us all, except for John, who was up an hour before our instructors came in to wake us. We ate a traditional breakfast on the island we now called home, then came the martial arts instructions.

"We started at the beginning. Our three teachers told us, you have never needed to learn to defend yourself or others." When the oldest of our instructors finished, I looked over to John.

John seemed to love this part of our day. Then, in the afternoon, we learned about the Jinn. What they were to that question, we learned they were where the myth or legend of the Jinn. In Arabic, they were called al-jinn. We in the western world call them genies, these creatures, these Jinn grant whatever the person wishes. The price for the wish is terrible; whoever summons these things must be insane.

Only John would be allowed to go with the others to hunt down a Jinn for the first years. Lisa, Jack, and I would stay up when he was gone worrying that our protector and friend would be hurt. While at the temple, I learned my father was forced to take my place, and the Jinn took his heart. My mother sent letters to the temple, and I was given each letter. I would stand in the garden looking at the envelope. I would turn it over in my hands, looking at it. Then drop the unopened letter into an incense burner and watch as the envelope slowly turns black and burns to ash. A light breeze would scatter what remained of the letters into the forest.

The small island bank and its monarch, who chose to help me, when I made good my escape from France, informed me my account had grown to a sizable fortune. I sent word I would like to keep it with them and make my investments as usual. On one of his trips, I asked John to go to the bank and thank the head of the bank for me. I sent a letter to the monarch with instructions if I was to pass away, that all my money was to be given to John. Of course, my friend and protector didn't know the contents of the letter. Once my father was killed by the dragons, my mother became head of the family. She made my father look like a saint. The order I was in had people all over the world. Word was sent to the temple that my mother had placed a one million dollar bounty on my and John's life. The order told me my mother wouldn't be able to pay the bounty in a year.

"Oh, she will be able to pay it, a million dollars is pocket change for my mother," I told the leader of our order.

"Yes, last year that would have been true, but the contract your ancestor made with the Jinn has been broken, so they took your father. Now they will take all they have been given, which means all the wealth your family has built will fall away. Your accounts will be safe due to the fact you started them yourself. The Jinn had nothing to do with your wealth." Huan said as we walked into the garden. Standing in the falling cherry blossoms, I thought about my sister. My so-called parents had sent me to the school before she was born; I never met her until she was four. The next time I saw her, she was twelve. It was this time she informed me I was not to stay long. She told me to see my father and then return to France, where I belong. She exploded when I laughed at her, and she started to say something when I turned and walked off. All I could think of was how she and my mother would handle being broke.

Jack and Lisa grew closer during our time in the temple, and by our third year, they were never apart. It was something to watch as their love for each other grew. Our lessons carried on every day. We were sitting at a late-night dinner with John as he told of the latest hunt.

"Well, when we finally found this one, she tried to bargain her way out of our grasp. She said she had information about Rod's mother." John told us.

"Well, what of Rod's mother, what's the news?" Jack asked.

"Well Rod, I don't know how to tell you this, the others and I struggled with how to best do this," John said as he looked at his plate. I thought he would tell me that the bitch had died or committed suicide.

"Just be straightforward, John; everything should be fine," I said, not being ready myself. John looked up and sighed, then told me what he and the others had found out.

"Your mother is insane. When the family fortune started to dwindle, and she realized the Jinn were taking it all back, she summoned them. She made another deal to restore the family fortune." John was telling us about the deal, and for some reason, I knew what was coming.

"The deal she made was to restore the fortune. She had to make a sacrifice; it was your little sister. The bitch gave your sixteen-year-old sister to them. The cunt cut out her own daughter's heart." John finished; I stood and walked out to the garden. I was walking down one of the paths built around the outside of the garden when I heard footsteps behind me. I knew it was the head of our order. He knew John told me what they had found out on the last outing.

"What are you feeling at this moment, Rod?" Huan asked from behind me. I stopped and looked into the stars of the night sky.

"At this moment, I'm feeling anger, hatred for my mother, and sadness for a young girl who was never given a chance to be good. She never had a chance to know there is more to life than money and power." I answered as I stood with my head tilted back then out of nowhere, I let loose a scream of hate and rage that startled me. I felt better when the scream subsided. Huan stepped beside me and patted my shoulder.

"It is better to get it all out now so that you will be clear-headed when you go on the next hunt." My teacher and the head of the unit said; I stood shocked it had been three years ago I walked up the path of the temple where my friends and I were to be trained.

"I am to go out on a hunt?" I asked, wondering if I had heard him correctly.

"Yes, I think you and the others are ready, and with this latest news, it will do you good to put what you've learned to use," Huan said as he turned and started back to the temple. I followed, still thinking about my sister, I had only met her twice, and she was a spoiled brat each time. I wanted to think when she got older that, she had become a friendly kid. That she wanted to see the world. A month later, I was shocked when a letter came to the temple for me. I thought it would be from my mother gloating about how she had kept the family fortune. It wasn't from my mother, it was from my sister. I stood in the garden and turned the letter over in my hands. The envelope shook as I held it in my unsteady hands, dreading what I would find written on the pages inside. This would be the first letter I opened. In the first line of her letter, she apologized for the last time she spoke to me. I smiled when she called herself a little shit. As I read the hurried writing on the paper, the pain started to ache in my chest. The words blurred as tears filled my eyes, as the first tear spilled over onto my cheeks. I could feel the heat of my rage trail to my chin, where my tears clung to my flesh.

"If you can, please come and get me away from mother. I think she is planning to kill me. I have run away and am hiding. I hope this letter finds you in time. I know we don't know each other, Rod, but please help me, save me. I'm so scared; I can see strangers prowling at night. I know they are looking for me. I dare not move. I paid a young boy to mail this for me. I pray it finds you in time. If it doesn't know, I had your pitcher next to my bed in my room; love your sister." I read and reread the last line of her letter. I could hear Lisa and Jack walking towards me in the garden.

"Did you get another letter from the egg donor?" Jack asked as a joke. I didn't turn around; I just handed Lisa the letter to read.

"Oh god, Rod, oh god, she wasn't like them; she ran like you. She was good," Lisa said as a tear rolled down her cheek. Jack stood with his arms wrapped around Lisa and me. I wanted to cry for my sister, but the rage aimed at my mother wouldn't let me grieve not until I avenged her murder. When John came to look for us, Lisa gave him the letter. I watched as our protector read my sisters' pleas for help, his big hands shaking with rage.

"That fucking monster hunted down her daughter and dragged her back for her rotten gains, Rod. I'm sorry, but I'm going to have to kill this bitch." John said as I looked at him.

"John, you'll be there, but if anybody is going to end that thing, it will be me. I feel it's my responsibility to rid the world of her," I said as John nodded.

"I understand, but I'm going to be right behind you the whole time," John told me. I nodded, thanking the lucky day this big man came back into my life.

The next night everyone in the temple had a silent ceremony for my sister. I wished I could have said anything about her. I looked at the wrinkled letter in my hand and decided to read it out loud for the others to hear how she had run, and in her last days, she was brave. When I was finished, I looked at the gathered members of our order.

"It's time I to go out and start hunting these things; we have got to rid our world of them. The first monster I need to be rid of is the thing that calls herself my mother." I watched as Huan and the other elders of the order spoke.

"It is time for you and your friends to start your hunt. There is another lesson you all need to learn before you head out; please follow us." Huan told us. As he and the others turned, we followed. We stopped at a small building; Lisa, Jack and I had been at the temple over the years. We each had seen the elders going into this small building. This was the first time we were to walk into the building. I was amazed to see the walls held paintings of many old men and women. In the centre of the building was a stairwell leading down; at the bottom, a gate was locked. The three of us were led to a table. We gathered around the small table while Huan took a book off a shelf.

"In this book are the names of families who have used the favour of the Jinn over the years. Some will come as a surprise, and others will not. It also gives the dates as far back as we can trace them. Now we don't know what will happen if we ever get to the point where we can kill the oldest of the Jinn. These families have been protecting the Jinn for the last three hundred years, so they are as responsible for the pain and suffering of the world as the beasts. Study these names, these families, keep them, make your own book and go out into the world knowing you are making it a better place for all."

When Huan finished, he placed the book on the table and opened it. Lisa turned the book and began reading it out loud. Our leader was right when he said we would be shocked. Lisa read the names of the most powerful families in the world. We wrote the names of the families down, then one by one and left the room under the temple.

Chapter 10

The first hunt took longer than I thought it would; we were sent to the Japanese mega city of Tokyo. We were forced to kidnap the father of a family whose name was in the book. John told us this is how we get the Jinn to send one of their protectors to us.

"Once the protector showed up, we kill the human; it's no great loss on humanity, then we grab the Jinn. Once we have the creature secure, we wait until a special unit of the order shows up, and they question it." John told us.

It took a week for the protector to show up. Unlike other times it was a pair, a male and female. I watched as the team walked down the street, they didn't know I could see their natural eyes, and as they walked past, I turned and walked back into the building where we were holding our first prisoner.

"Well, they are here, a male and a female," I told the others. We knew the Jinn couldn't get into the building without us knowing. John made sure traps were set at every entry point. John turned and looked at the man tied to the chair; we knew about this man. He sacrificed his oldest son to the Jinn just to retain his wealth and power within the Japanese government. John walked over to him and patted his shoulder.

"Well, you shit, it looks like they've come to save you." Then before the man could mumble anything through his gag, John pulled his knife and ran the razor-sharp blade across the man's throat. Lisa, jack and

I watched as the man's blood splashed across the floor as his heart pumped the blood out of his body.

"The smell of his blood will bring those two Jinns crashing in here, so get ready," John warned us. He was right. A few moments later, we heard a crash at the back of the building. A second after the crash, we listened to a window being smashed out in the front of the building. John whispered for us to wait, to let them make the first move.

"Trust in our traps; trust in each other." He whispered. The female was the first one to make it to the back room. When she rounded the corner and saw the dead body of the man she was to retrieve, she looked at the four of us, and something between a low growl and a hiss escaped from her. She was slowly walking into the room when a heavy board loaded with spikes dropped from the ceiling and impaled her. Jack and I ran to her and wrapped ropes around her and the board, tying her to the floor. Then we heard another trap go off in the building, and a scream came from the other room.

"It's trying to bait us into leaving our safe room, smart for a thing," John said loud enough for it to hear.

"Fuck you, human. I'm going to eat well tonight." The Jinn said from the hallway.

"Well, come and see what's on the menu, you fowl thing," I said before I could stop myself. John smiled at me. I cocked the Remington street sweeper shotgun I was holding. Before I knew what was going on, the large male Jinn was standing in the doorway looking at the dead body of his ward and the female Jinn tied to a board she was impaled on. The beast was about to say something when I squeezed the trigger on the shotgun. The slug tore through his thigh, smashing the bone to power, and great gouts of bloody purple meat hit the wall behind the creature. It started to crawl into the room, trying to get at me. I smiled as I ran at the beast holding a sword. As I jumped over the thing crawling on the floor, I drove the blade of the sword through its back, pinning it to the floor. Lisa and Jack did the same, effectively stopping all movement from the creature. We turned and watched as John took out his phone and hit a number, then waited. Someone answered and then hung up without saying a word. John smiled, then walked over to the dead man and covered the body.

I was shocked when another team arrived in less than an hour. the second team moved in and started to question the two Jinn. The body of the man John killed was taken and dissolved in acid, then burned, and the ashes were to be spread in a landfill. The team worked on the Jinn for two days until they got the answers they needed. Then, those two were killed and dissolved and burned.

"With the Jinn, you must dissolve the body, or they will heal and come back; it must be destroyed on a cellar level." One of the interrogators told us. I didn't care. I was happy with the thought there were two fewer things in the world, two fewer and who knew how many left to go.

We never went back to the temple on the island of Shikotan. Instead, Lisa, Jack, John, and I returned to France. To another of the sacred temples the Jinn couldn't enter, one man stood at the gates and smiled at us as we stepped through.

"It is so good to see young people again; it is so sad that you have to carry the burden of this fight." He said as he looked at Lisa.

"We must save others like us from the greed of their families," Lisa said as she stood in front of the keeper of the Dome du Gouter temple in the French alps.

"Here you will be safe." Our brother assured us as he ushered our party of four into the temple courtyard.

"This temple was set up by a pope several centuries ago. He knew about the beasts. This pope ordered the hunting and destruction of the Jinn down to the last one."

"Why has it taken so long for us to be rid of the Jinn?" Jack asked.

"Well, it has to do with the families, they so covet their power and wealth that they protect the beasts, and they think nothing of giving one of their sons over to them. Now your grandfather was a strong man with a stronger son, little sister." Our brother told Lisa as she blushed.

"I know; I just wish I could have met my grandfather. I know him from pictures and how my grandmother spoke about him." Our friend said as a tear rolled from the corner of her eye. That night we sat talking about the fathers who defied the Jinns' deal of taking their sons. These men have given their lives up, along with their family's power. The following weeks were spent learning of families who would be our allies and those who would give anyone of us to the beasts. I wasn't surprised to hear my family name at the top of the later list. After all, my mother had killed my little sister to keep her wealth and power.

"And about your mother, she has hired a south African mercenary crew to hunt you down. She knows it's too late to save your father, she is hunting you down to kill you, and unlike the Jinn, these men can walk right into the temples." Gerard told us as we sipped tea.

"So what are we going to do about it," I asked, looking at the others.

"We are going to take them; we are going to educate the men she hires. Once they know the truth, we'll set them free. They will tell others soon she'll have to rely on her security staff." John told us.

Chapter 11

The following year was filled with us hunting our main target, the Jinn. We captured the first South African team my mother hired. We showed their leader a Jinn and explained everything about them. How they have been manipulating power and wealth throughout the world for centuries. All but one of the first teams joined the order and took up the hunt for the Jinn.

The fact that her first team failed and, worse, joined me in the order didn't hinder my mother in her quest to have me brought to her dead. She used her power and wealth to hire more teams, and as we learned about these teams, we would set traps for them. I didn't want to kill these men and women. I wanted to talk to them to see if we could bring them into our order. The men and women who had served in the military would see they could again do good service and would join us. As for the others, they were strictly in it for the money. These others John would transport these to a secret location with our brother Gerard. Lisa, Jack, and I never really knew what happened to them. The months turned into years; the whole time we hunted the Jinn, we would also receive information about people my mother would hire to kill John and me. So we would study and set traps for my mother's teams of mercenaries. I could hardly believe six years had passed since the day I ran over the mountains in the south of France. We had trapped dozens of Jinn to be questioned, and the team who always did interviews told us the Jinn the order had been killing were getting older and older.

"Have we killed all the younger ones?" I asked, hoping we were starting to see results in our quest.

"Well, it's hard to tell. It could be the older ones are trying to protect the younger ones from us." One of the interrogators told us the leader of the interrogation team smiled.

"That's a good thing. If the older ones are coming out of hiding to protect the younger Jinn and the families, then it means you have them scared." The lead integrator said as they finished packing their equipment and turned to leave.

"I know you guys want to keep hunting, Jinn. For me, I think it's time for the bitch who calls herself my mother to answer for killing my sister and god knows how many more," I said as I turned and looked at the others.

"I agree with Rod; it will send a clear message to the other families. The Jinn can't protect them," John said as he sat down. We started to plan the kidnapping of my mother, but we still hunted the Jinn. However, all our free time was spent gathering information on the bitch and her security team.

"Well, she is spending her money wisely; her team is airtight. The only way we will get near her is in the air. It's something I still don't understand." John was saying as he looked over the latest batch of intel gathered by our sources.

"What's the problem?" I asked as I walked into the room.

"Your crazy ass mother has one of the best security teams in the business; she is fully protected until she boards your father's jet. She never lets them on the jet. Her security team flies to wherever she is going on a second jet." John told me as he showed me the pictures of her flying out by herself. I smiled and looked at the pictures; if we were going to do this, we would have to do it in the air.

"I would love to know what the hell she is trying to hide from her team. You don't think she has a Jinn with her on that plane, do you?" I asked John, who looked up from the information packet.

"Well, I never thought of that. It would explain why your mother refuses to allow her team on the plane. Ok, our first priority is to ascertain what the hell she is hiding on her plane; it has to be something so important she would put her security at risk to hide. While we're doing that, we'll need another team to monitor the bitch so we can nail down her movements." John was in full gear now. I stood at his side and watched him work.

"The only thing we have to be careful of is tipping her off, so we will have teams set up in different countries around the world. That way, she never sees the same faces. We won't have them in every country she travels to. This will take time; we will have to work on this slowly. It might take more than a year to get it all nailed down, Rod; you ok with that?" John asked me.

"If we are doing something, then I can see the end to that thing's life," I answered my friend and protector.

It took almost a year for John to have his teams in place. He had gone to each country where John wanted a team and had found men and women who had at one time worked in the security service of that country and whose families had been affected by the Jinn. Once he had proven the beasts were real, John explained what my mother had done to her children. Those men and women were more than eager to help with intel gathering. While John was out gathering his teams together, Jack, Lisa and I were hunting. On our third hunt, we caught a very old Jinn.

The beast was walking down a darkened street, its cane tapping on the sidewalk. Jack darted the thing causing it to turn around; Lisa dropped a net over it from her perch on a balcony. Once it was on the ground, I ran up and injected a sedative that would've been fatal for a human. The interrogation team was on its way, and Lisa, Jack and I ensured we were secured. Then before the interrogation team arrived, the thing we had captured started to speak.

"Hello Rod, we hear that is what you call yourself. Is it that you hate your now-dead father so much that you can't use his name? Or do you think it sounds cool, as you kids say?" It hissed at me; I stood shocked the thing knew my name.

"Nice parlour trick, so you know my name," I said and acted board.

"It is no parlour trick, my boy; you were to be mine." It hissed. I could see the hate in its eyes.

"Oh, well, sorry about that. I had other plans, and being killed for some old beast wasn't in them." I smiled at the nasty thing.

"Do you know what you've done? Your greed has killed your father and your young sister?" Lisa reached up and placed her hand on my shoulder to keep me calm. I knew it was trying to get me enraged, hoping I'd make a mistake. I smiled at Lisa and Jack to let them know I was alright. I wanted answers more than the gratification of killing this thing.

The interrogation team was with us for a week; they worked around the clock on the Jinn. The information they learned shocked us all. The old Jinn finally broke down and told of how their numbers were slowly dwindling. It seems our order was indeed winning the war with them. Now the old ones were forced to come out and gather their sacrifices. The one Lisa, Jack and I grabbed was there to collect a young man in the hope of extending his life. We discovered that when a sacrifice runs, the Jinn who was to get his heart loses some of its own heart and life force. I had asked the interrogation team to ask one question for me before it was killed. I wanted to know if my sisters' soul was trapped in one of them.

"I asked your question, Rod; the Jinn assures me your sister couldn't be used. They made your mother kill your sister to prove her worth." I was told by the leader of the team. We went into the room with the body of the old Jinn and watched as it was submerged in a barrel of acid. Once the body was dissolved, we took the sludge to a landfill, and with the aid of gas and diesel, we burned the sludge. That night I sat under a large oak tree and looked up into the starry firmament. I wished I could have known my sister; I felt a tear roll down my cheek.

The following day I found John sitting at the table in our temple; he smiled at me as I walked in.

"Well, good morning, stranger," I said as I sat.

"Well, it is a good morning. I heard you guys caught a good one while I was gone," John told me as he stirred his coffee.

"Yeah, we learned a lot from the old thing. It told us the young ones have all been wiped out by us and others of our order. Now the old ones need to go out and gather their sacrifices. Also, I found out my sister wasn't used by any of the Jinn. My mother killed her to prove to them she was willing to do anything to retain the power and wealth." I finished as John placed a cup of coffee in front of me.

"Well, I have news on the bitch front, it has taken some time, but we have found a pattern to her movements. We have her travelling to the same spot in Patagonia, for what we don't have a clue." John told me as Jack walked into the kitchen.

"Whose in Patagonia? There ain't much there, but it is beautiful," Jack said as he sat down with his coffee.

"It's my mother; she has taken an interest in the area," I said.

"Well, that's the shits for those people," Jack said as he sipped from the steaming cup. Lisa stood at the door looking at the three of us, shaking her head.

"So what's the plan to rid the world of the thing that dares calls itself a mother?" She asked as she took Jack's cup of coffee and stole a sip.

"Well, that's the thing, we'll have to come up with a plan, then we'll have to refine it until we have one that will work. Because if we miss the first time, we'll never get another chance." John told us.

"Are we still working on the lack of security on her plane?" Jack asked. We turned and looked at him, knowing he was about to start us off on the planning.

"Yes, I think that would be the best place to do anything," John said as he poured Lisa a cup of coffee.

"I know you have a plan in mind, buddy; what is it, and how crazy is it?" John asked.

"Well, it's pretty far out there. I was thinking of taking out the bitches whole plane," Jack told us. I turned and looked at John, who shrugged his big shoulders.

"What do you mean take out her whole plane, and what about the pilots and other people she has on it?" I asked, hoping Jack had thought about them.

"Oh, I wouldn't worry about them," John stated from the fridge. Lisa turned and looked at him for a second.

"The people she has on the plane with her are all Jinn, though I don't think she knows they are all Jinn. She seems to only know about one of them, and it's the one who killed your father. I think she might be the oldest of them and the one who started this whole goddamn mess." John told us.

"Ok, so this is what I was thinking; we have a plane staged someplace in the Patagonian desert waiting for her next trip." Jack started.

For the next week, we looked at our plan repeatedly, trying to find its flaw before we locked everything in. We kept hunting as our plan came together; we found and captured four older Jinn. Once the interrogation unit was done and had gathered all the information they could, we destroyed the bodies and moved on. Eight months passed, and our plan was set; we had found and bought the plane Jack said he would need for the job. John purchased the rifle he would need, the ammunition he wanted to load himself. Intel came in that my mother was going to take another trip to Patagonia. However, unlike the previous trips, we knew this one would be her last. Jack and John flew to the end of the world ahead of my mother's trip to set everything up. Lisa and I, along with the interrogation team, chartered a plane and flew into Balmaceda airport, which served Coyhaique Aysen Region. This airstrip was 4 kilometres from the border with Argentina. From this point, we rented 2 SUVs and started into the mountains of Patagonia.

Kaia, the interrogation team leader, and I sat next to each other as our group made its way through the mountains. We stopped to make camp on top of a pass one night. After our meal, I sat on a rock overlooking a valley. I couldn't help but think of my sister. Did she ever get to see anything like this before she was murdered? The Jinn said they couldn't use her. Was that because she was a girl, or did she find love? I had so many questions, and the one person who could answer my questions, I came to the end of the world to kill. Kaia walked over to where I was sitting. She looked down into the valley, then up into the most beautiful night sky we had ever seen.

"Do you think about your mother?" She asked.

"No, I was thinking of my sister. I was wondering if she ever saw a sky like this before she was murdered," I said.

"It is a nice thing to think she did," Kaia said as she sat beside me. We didn't speak for some time. It was nice to sit and be with another person; the fact she was beautiful made it better. I knew Lisa was watching from her tent; I knew she was hoping I would find someone to love. I told Lisa years ago I couldn't let anyone get close to me until this part of my life was over. The next few days, Kaia and I grew closer. I found myself looking for her before we ate. I would miss her when I would sit and watch the stars show themselves as the day surrendered to the night. It was the afternoon of the sixth day when we arrived at the geographical longitude and latitude John and Jack gave us before they left to scout around.

At first, Lisa and I thought something had gone wrong. We couldn't see anything like a camp or any indication our two friends were there. Kaia walked around with Lisa looking at the ground, trying to pick up a sign John or Jack had been there. I was about to say we should get the gear out and start a search for our friends when I heard Lisa shout. Turning, I watched as she ran for a figure, slowly solidifying out of the desert heat. It didn't take too long after she jumped into the arms of the figure. I realized it had to be Jack.

"This is some base you and John made," I said as I stood in the large cave housing our plane and camp.

"Before John and I landed, he saw a deep shadow; when we explored it, we found this cave. It seemed to be calling to us, so we set everything up here." Jack explained as we looked around the base.

"Also, John thinks he knows what your mother and the Jinn have been up to down here," Jack added.

"Where is John? I would have thought he would've been here when we arrived?" Lisa asked as she looked the plane over.

"He's looking over the site your mother, and the Jinn have been building. It's a mine, though nothing is being mined." Jack told us. I was about to ask another question when we heard John arriving. He smiled as we walked out of the cave to greet him.

"You all made it; that's great. We have some work to finish before we're ready. I got to get a closer look at what the bitch and the beasts are up to at that old mine." John informed us Kaia stepped forward when John mentioned the mine.

"Could you tell me so we can add this to our knowledge of them, please?" She asked as we all walked back into the cave.

"Sure, but first, let's eat, then we'll talk." We sat and had a dinner of heated military ready-to-eat meals. Surprisingly they were pretty good.

"Ok, Jack and I have been watching the site the bitch bought. It's an old gold mine. It runs into a mountain from a flat plain the same as ours here, but unlike ours, it has been outfitted with lab equipment."

John told us as the interrogation team made notes. I could see the news; these Jinn and my mother were bringing lab equipment that bothered Kaia and her team. I was about to ask what they thought she could be up to when Jack continued where John had left off.

"We wondered what the hell they were up to. We watched and couldn't believe our eyes when another plane landed at their field."

"Both Jack and I were there when they wheeled a Jinn off the plane. He wasn't going willingly; the thing was throwing a fit. They used some kind of dart. Once the beast was out, he was wheeled into their base. For what we don't know, now that you guys are here, we can find out." John finished.

"After we kill my mother and whatever else is on the plane with her," I added, knowing we only had fourteen days before she arrived.

Chapter 12

Two weeks passed quickly, for some of us too quickly. We had finished all the modifications to the plane Jack wanted. The biggest one was the firing port where John could set himself up to take out the engines of my mother's plane. With no power source, it would force her to the ground on our terms. We wouldn't have to worry about her security team. The order had found out when she travelled down here she never used her security team.

The day arrived, and I watched as the radar on our plane swept the sky, looking for another plane. I could feel my trepidation starting to climb in me. I began to think the monster and the Jinn she travelled with somehow found out what we were doing. I was about to rage about the wasted time when the radar chirped, and a few seconds later, it chirped again.

"There she is," Jack said as he pointed to the radar screen. I wanted to run back and tell John. I knew he had already had the plane in his scope. John's first shot took out the ability of the pilots to call for help his second and third destroyed the engines on my mother's plane. I watched as our target started to sink toward the hard-packed desert floor. When the pilots lowered the jet's landing gear, John aimed and destroyed the nose gear and the left gear under the wing. I watched as my mother looked out the window, panic etched across her face. I smiled and waved at her. I didn't think she could see me until she started pounding on her window with her fists. I smiled at the woman who thought nothing of her children, the creature who had killed her daughter for wealth. As I watched the jet sink towards the earth, I realized I felt a peace flow over me. My mother's jet glided to the floor of the desert; for a second, it looked as if her pilots were going to be able to bring it in without losing control. When the landing gear on the left side of the jet touched down, it dug in, causing the plane to swing sideways. The rush started to roll its wings shearing off, and the cockpit and tail section broke off, rolling off in different directions. The main body of my mother's jet rolled, throwing debris all over the place. Jack landed and taxied to a stop fifty feet from the wreckage. We were only twenty-five miles from our base.

"Ok, check your weapons and move together. We don't know how many survived, so assume they all did," John told us as we stepped onto the desert floor. John taught us how to move through a combat zone, and we use those lessons now. As we approached the downed leer jet, we could hear movement from inside. Circling wide, we broke into two teams, one heading for the front of the wreckage and the other towards the rear. When I rounded the front of the wreck, I found one of the Jinn crawling out. It looked up and hissed. I put two rounds from my Mp5 through its head. Most of the beasts were dead. We know if we left them, they would come back to life. So we gathered the bodies and shot each one through the head, then added fuel to the bodies and burned them. John found my mother. She was tangled in the wreckage, and it took us some time to get her out. We had her in the shade of the wing of our plane, her legs were broken, and from the sound of her breathing, she had internal injuries. I was sitting in front of her when she woke up. I had a smile on my face when she realized I had her.

"Well, the egg donor is awake," I called to the others; I could tell she knew I called her the egg donor instead of mother to others.

"You have destroyed everything, you had one purpose in this life, and you couldn't do that." She said.

"Yes, I had one purpose, to live, you see you incept bitch I was born to see the end of these monsters, along with you and the others like you who serve them." I could see the pain written on her face. Now I need to know whether you murdered my sister, your little girl. Or did she get away from you and the things you covet?" I watched as a smile tugged at the corners of her lips.

"No, she didn't get away; we found her. She begged and cried, that's what you fucking kids don't understand. We have been chosen by god herself for this." Sitting in front of my mother, I couldn't believe her level of bat shit crazy.

"So, like me, my sister wanted to live. She wanted to fall in love, to become a mother, to see her children grow, to travel the world, make friends sit and watch the sunsets holding the hand of that special person in her life. Then you and that fucking nitwit father of ours and your insane greed took that from her. You murdered your own daughter." I could see my words were having an effect on the bitch. Then she looked at me and smiled.

"You killed your father and your sister when you ran." I slowly stood up; I just shook my head as I looked down at her. I could have argued with her. I could have told her murdering her child for gain was the ultimate wrong. Instead, I just shook my head at the evil in front of me. I was about to turn away, and for a moment, I could see hope blossoming in my mothers' eyes. I shot my egg donor between the eyes, the 9mm round punching a neat round hole in her forehead. What was left of my mother's brain sprayed across the ground staining the desert hardpan.

Turning, I found John standing behind me; he had kept his word and stood behind me the whole time. The rest of the team stood and nodded, knowing I did the right thing and just killed the bitch outright. John and I took my mother's body and threw it on the burning bodies of the Jinn. We added more fuel. Once the bodies were burned to ash, the interrogation team took the time to gather them so we could spread them from the plane as we flew to the mine my mother bought.

Landing at the former mine site, now turned secret evil lair of my mother's, was easier than any of us thought. There was very little in the way of security at the landing strip. That all changed when we made our way to the main mine site. Five security guards met us with automatic weapons and tried to stop us. We didn't want to hurt them if they were human. After getting a good look at the men, I informed the others they were all Jinn. John threw a grenade into their security shack, forcing them to vacate their shelter. Within minutes of the grenade explosion, the five guards were dead. The interrogation team cut off their heads to stop them from healing too fast.

"We'll have to come back and gather the bodies to destroy them when we are finished," Kaia told us; we all nodded, moving further into the mine-turned-lab. As we moved further underground, we found the only security at the site were the five we had killed at the top. The only ones in the labs were Jinn, involved with the experiments, those we killed after the interrogation team finished with them.

"They all say the same thing; they are trying to find a way to breed a hybrid. A cross between a Jinn and a human, the Jinn they brought here against its will, has something to do with it." Kaia told us.

"Well, let us go and find this special Jinn and see if we can get the answers we need," Jack said as he stepped into an elevator. The lower levels were the same as the upper ones, just lab after lab. I thought it would take more than a day to search the whole complex. It seemed we would never find this mysterious Jinn who held the answers we needed. John whistled from the doorway of another lab; he smiled at us as we turned.

"I do believe this chap is being held against his will, as they say," John said as I joined him. In the centre of the lab was the Jinn we were looking for. John had killed the technician before any of us could react.

"So what did you do to end up in this state?" I asked this, Jinn.

"I dared to think for myself." The thing stated. Lisa walked into the room with Kaia. When the Jinn on the table recognized the leader of the interrogation team, I could see real fear in its eyes.

"You can talk to all of us, or you can talk to her team alone; it's up to you," I told the beast. It took less than a second for the creature to make up his mind.

"I hold no loyalty to the queen or her ilk. Ask what you will I'll answer. However, when I answer your last question, promise me you'll end my life as a kindness."

"I give you my word; I'll do you that one kindness," I promised. Then before I or any of you could ask a question, the Jinn started to speak.

"I was trapped in the mountains on a peninsula in Russia's far east. I spent many years there hibernating when I was forced to wake up due to hunger. I met a blind woman who lived by herself. She helped me, and over the years, we grew close, so we had a child." It told us Lisa and Kaia reacted when the Jinn told us it had fathered a child with a human woman.

"We know your kind don't or can't mate with humans; most certainly, our biology isn't compatible to breed with each other," Lisa said as she looked through some paperwork on the desk.

"I tell the truth, Alexandria did indeed have a child, though the poor boy only lived for a few weeks. He was my son. I held and loved him; when he died, his mother took her life the next day. I buried them together, hoping whatever happens to humans when they die, they would be together." The Jinn told those of us who gathered around the lab.

"So why did they drag you here?" Jack asked.

"I left Russia and came down here, hoping to be alone to die. When the queen heard one of us had a child with a human, she wanted it to happen again. The queen and her scientists wanted to perfect it, so she could have a slave race."

"The queen, this isn't the first time I've heard of this queen," Kaia told us.

"So there is one who is the leader of all of you?" John asked the Jinn.

"Yes, she is our queen, you could say. She is the one who ordered your mother to kill your sister." I raised my Mp5 and placed the barrel on the forehead of the dragon.

"If you've been gone for so long, how in the hell do you know about that?" I asked as I started to take up trigger slack.

"My kind is always in contact with the queen if we want it. It's the only freedom we have from her." It told me.

"What does that mean? It's the only freedom?" Lisa asked from the computer.

"If you were to let me go, and if I was found and taken to her, I would have no choice but to answer all her questions. Also, once back with her, I would be made to start hunting your order again." This trapped Jinn told us.

"So she has complete control over your kind, except you can close her out of your mind." Kaia reiterated.

"Yes, but only from a distance, if I was close to her, I couldn't keep her out, she would know everything. Before you leave, you have to gather all their work and stop them. You can not fail, or it will mean the end of the human race. The elder wishes to bring more of our kind here." The Jinn told us I could see the fear in its eyes. It wasn't the fear of us or of dying. It seemed to be afraid more of its kind would arrive.

"Bring more of your kind here; from where, where is it you come from?" John asked

"We come from another plain of existence, our leaders sent the queen here to be rid of her evil. Then the next groups sent here were criminals where I come from. The others, including myself, were sent after her. Once the freedom leaders realized this world was inhabited, they knew the gate had to be closed. Some of us wanted to go back. However, the queen was determined to stay and gain control of this world." The tortured Jinn told us. I wondered how the hell the queen, as he called it, could influence people.

"How is she able to control people, to get them to do what she wants?" I asked, needing to know.

"That's the easiest part for her. If a person has a weak mind, she can bend their will to do what she wants. I hate to say it, but most of your richest families and royalty have suffered from incest and inbreeding, so she can force her will on them." The wretched creature told us.

"Ok, so why the killing of a son? What the hell does she get from that?" Lisa asked before I could.

"Where I come from, the queen was tried and convicted of murdering her family, along with scores of others. In our ancient past our race was cannibals, my race has left that in past. However, the queen discovered that if she ate the heart of the family's offspring, she would gain life force. Most of those who follow her also eat of the heart. They get years added to their life with it, though she controls who gets what heart." We stood shocked by what we heard. Now we know about the life force. What surprised us was the queen, and the others were from a parallel universe.

"Where is this gate you spoke of?" Kaia asked.

"The gate we came through was in the catacombs of Paris. When the queen landed, the city was in the grip of the plague. She has worked on building the empire you see today; the families she controls will do anything to keep what she has given them. Wars have been started and fought over her favour, you have to kill her or get her to the gate."

"Why the gate?" John asked.

"If you can get her to the gate, then the leaders from my world will know she is nearby. They will open the gate and take her back by force. Now before you go, please kill me, I don't want to go back to my world, and I don't have the heart to live here any longer." It begged us as I looked at the tormented thing lying strapped to the table in front of us. I never realized I had raised my Mp5. The Jinn smiled at me and whispered a thank you before the 9 mm round entered its skull killing it, if only temporarily.

"We need to find acid and dissolve the body of this Jinn," John told us as we turned to leave the room. We did the same to the others we had killed earlier. Then we found a massive store of military-grade explosives, John, Jack and I rigged the explosives to implode the mine so it could never be used again. Three days later as I and the others flew over Mexico, I was informed my mother's plane was missing and a search had been started. I thanked the official from the Argentinean government and asked him to keep in contact with me. Good to his word, the man called me every day for the first while, then once a week. One day I received a call; the search had been called off. A new official from the Argentinean government informed me bits of the wreckage were located, and she was presumed dead. It was then a herd of lawyers started calling. Seeing I was the only heir to the family fortune they wanted a share of it. It seemed to put them off when I told them the whole thing would be donated to a charity of my choice. Good to my word, I broke the fortune up and donated it. The lions share going to the order I'm a part of so we could keep the hunt for the elder Jinn.

Chapter 13

We targeted the families who use the queen and her power for their gain. We didn't go and kill the families. Instead, we found where these families started to hide their sons. Though it was technically kidnapping we would take the sons of the families to the temples. We taught them about their families and what the future holds for them. Then we give them the choice to be a sacrifice or to live. The unit never had a son who wanted to be sacrificed, not one. One by one, the families started falling by the wayside. Without massive donations to political parties, most of the corruption in governments worldwide started to dwindle. The power-mad decided if they couldn't steal vast amounts of the taxpayer's money, then it wasn't worth begging to be voted in and left. The good people in the governments did what they were intended for; they started to work for the people.

John, Lisa, Jack and I wandered around the catacombs under Paris trying to find anything that would give us a clue about where the gate was. I was about to give up when we heard a high pitch whine; it sounded like a turbine jet engine. The sound echoed around the catacombs for a few minutes and stopped before we could find what was causing the sound.

"Do you think that sound had anything to with the gate the Jinn spoke about?" Jack asked as we stood at a junction, each of us looking down a different hallway. I was about to joke about how this would be when a bad guy would show up. I turned and smiled at Jack when the sound started again; we could tell it was closer than before. Looked at each other, then we looked down the right-hand tunnel and started to run. We knew finding the origin of the sound would bring us to the gate the Jinn spoke of in Patagonia.

Jack and I stopped when we came to a spot of distortion in the tunnel; we couldn't see anything past the distortion. The sound coming from it was almost unbearable, for brief instances something on the other side could be made out. I stepped forward, wanting to step through the distortion, I wondered where it would take me, and John reached out and stopped me.

"The hell do you think you're doing, Rod?" He asked, knowing the answer.

"Well, I was going to see where that leads to," I answered pointing to the gate when a voice came through it. The voice was hard to make out over the sound of the gate. Lisa pulled her phone out and started to record the voice. Then as quickly as the gate opened, it closed just as the voice stopped.

"Ok, let's get the hell out of here," Jack said to all of us, nodding. It took us the rest of the day to find our way out of the catacombs. Once we reached the streets overhead the first thing we did was grab some take-out, then we raced back to the temple. Kaia was worried about us. She seemed to be more concerned about me, and she wouldn't leave my side all night. I held her hand and sat closer to her. I was surprised when she would brush up against me. To my annoyance, Lisa and John would smile and wink at me whenever Kaia would leave the room. Jack was, as usual, blind to everything except for Lisa and his plane. The feelings I had for Kaia grew and grew to my shock. I found I hated being away from her. When I was at the temple, I wanted to spend every second with her. The equipment we had at the temple was basic stereo and couldn't filter out to sound of the distortion. Looking at each other, we knew the equipment we would need to buy.

A week later, we turned one of the smaller rooms of the temple into a sound studio. That night we all sat in the room and waited for Jack to filter the distortion noise out of the recording; what we heard shocked us all.

As far as we could tell it was the voice of what we called a Jinn, it seemed to be filtered through water. Though we all were sure, it was the distortion of the voice coming from a parallel universe.

"If you on the other side can hear us, we will have someone at this place in thirty of your days. We want to take our criminals back. We are so sorry for any harm she and others like her have wreaked on your world. It was not our intention to harm your world." The others in the recording said then the message was repeated in french, then again in Spanish.

"Well, there you have it, they want them back. Do you think they'll be upset we've killed most of them off?" John asked.

"I don't know. I just wonder how we get the queen there, then give her back to them?" Jack asked. All I could think of at this point was this could all be over in one month. Standing around the temple, we looked at each other, trying to think of anything we could use to accomplish our task.

The next thirty days flew past as the unit hunted for the queen. Good to their word, the Jinn from the other side made contact. We stood at the point where we had seen the gate before. At 6 pm, the gate opened with the sound of a jet engine. This time we sent a message to the other side.

Well, we hoped they had gotten it; we told them we would try and have the elder at this point in thirty days. Lisa had been recording the whole time. When we returned to the temple, we were shocked to hear they had sent us a message.

"We will be sending a small group of our law officers to aid in the capture of our former queen. They will help you rid your world of her insanity." Again the voice ended as the gate closed. Different units from around the world hunted the world over trying to find the queen. Our unit worked, trying to see where the queen was hiding. In the evenings, it seemed all we could speak of was finally our world would be rid of the queen and the evil she had spread.

"If we could only find her, there has to be a family or place we haven't found yet. One the order doesn't know about, could there have been a family hidden from the order?" I asked one night as Kaia, and I stood looking at the northern lights dance across the arctic sky.

"There could be, I guess, the order was pretty diligent in keeping up to date with the families, though," Kaia said as we stood holding hands under the fantastic display of nature's beauty. That was the first night Kaia stood on her tiptoes and kissed me, then she turned and walked into the hotel lobby. Turning, I looked up into the sky, knowing I was falling in love for the first time in my life. I smiled at the waving bands of greens and blues as the lights grew brighter. I knew my sister would have been happy for me. I so desperately wanted her to be with me. To know her, to see her smile, to hear her laugh. She and other innocents had been ripped from this world, from their lives for nothing so needless as greed, and power. As I turned to walk back to the hotel lobby, I was surprised to see Kaia waiting for me by the door. It was then I looked up and found Lisa and John smiling at me from a balcony. I looked up at them, and to Lisa's shock, I flipped them the bird and laughed. That night was the greatest night of my life, Kaia and I found love with each other. With the softest touch, and gentle kisses we found peace and love. That was the night I needed all this to be over, not for myself, but for everything. This world of ours was never meant to be ruled over by a few who have no morals, no soul, and those who will murder their children to keep that power. When I left the school, I knew I would die before I found love. I had convinced myself of that, but as I watched Kaia sleep, I knew I had been wrong. I had found my love, the one I wanted to spend the rest of my life with.

As the sun rose over the snow, I looked forward to my future. I wanted to grow old. I never told anyone, especially my friends, but for some time, I was looking forward to the end of the Jinn. So I could go to a part of the world no one knew about. When I found the place I was looking for, I would call Lisa, Jack and John, and I would tell them I loved them. When I knew my real family was set up with the wealth I had, I would end my life. Instead, thirty days later, Lisa Jack, John and I were waiting at the point in the Paris catacombs where the gate to the other place would open.

Chapter 14

We were shocked by the small contingent that came through the gate. They were just as shocked by us as we were by them. The leader of the Jinn stepped forward and introduced himself and his team. We did the same and shook hands with the team from the other side. John and I couldn't get over the almost seven-foot-tall Jinn from the other side. These law officers seemed just as shocked at our size as we were at theirs. These Jinns did nothing to hide what they looked like.

Mostly, they looked like a human except for etchings that marked their pale blue skin. Each Jinn had different markings. It was like a fingerprint covering their entire body. Their leader explained it was how at one time in their past, a caste system was set up to make sure there was always a slave population. We all were shocked as we made our way out of the catacombs; the new Jinn slowly changed their appearance. By the time we found the exit and were standing in the sunshine of a Paris afternoon, the Jinn looked taller than us. We never wasted any time getting going on the hunt. With the aid of our friends from the other world, we found the queen on month six. She had mercenary teams each time we saw her teams, we would try to capture them so they could learn the truth. For most, this was enough for them to leave her. For the others, the draw of her money kept them. It was these men and women we were forced to kill when we found the queen in the Azores. While our team was forced to fight the queen's security.

The youngest of the Jinn was shot and killed for a short time. I watched as his team leader injected the young Jinn with something. When I asked what it was, he told me it was medicine to slow the healing process.

"I don't understand why you would want to slow it down?" I asked.

"We slow the healing down so he will heal as he was; if allowed to heal quickly, he would need to feed to replace vital nutrients. Slowing this down means he will be better off in the long run." When the team leader finished, we went to check on the others. Jack had a broken leg, and Lisa was looking after him. John and the other Jinn watched as a private jet lifted into the sky.

"Well, she got away; now, where the hell will she go, and how long will it take for us to find her?" John asked, but no one answered; we all felt the same. Again our team, along with the Jinn, hunted their former queen. We knew she would be harder to find now. The temple in France we called home felt empty with Jack and Lisa back in Japan.

Jack's leg needed surgery to repair the bone damage, and Lisa wouldn't leave his side. Kaia stayed with me, and we walked the grounds of the temple hand in hand every night. Six more months passed with no word on the queen; one of the Jinn joked he hoped her plane crashed.

I was losing hope we would ever see her again, then word came to our order the queen had been seen in Namibia. As we looked over the intel, none of us could have guessed what the queen was doing in the African country. I felt this was something we desperately needed to check on. I remembered the mine in Patagonia and the Jinn who told us of her plans. We have to find out what the hell she is up to, she could still be working on having a half-breed program. John and the leader of the Jinn team worked on planning our incursion into Namibia. Thirty days later, our plane set down on a private runway operated by a closed gold mine in Namibia's hot, dusty country. John taxied our aircraft to the closest building. For a moment, we thought there wasn't anyone around. Then before anyone could speak a hail of gunfire slammed the side of our plane. John pushed the throttles forward on the plane pulling around the first building for cover. The whole team was out and in a fire line when security ran around the building into our deadly fire. As far as we could tell all the security were human, all but one; the leader of this security team was a Jinn. The leader of our Jinn team didn't waste any time. He used his weapon to disintegrate the security Jinn.

We met resistance as we entered the main building of the mine. Though most gave up when the Jinn started to fire their weapons. I was shocked when one Jinn, who was fighting to keep us out of the mine, stood and ran screaming. I looked at the Jinn team leader questioningly, wondering what the hell it was screaming.

"Back in our world, this unit is only sent to capture the very worst of criminals. The ones we hunt have been found guilty of the worst crimes in our world, and their sentence is death. This is a sentence our elders only use in the most abhorrent of cases; we are called reapers in your language." The leader told us as a unit, we moved forward. Once we started down into the mine itself, resistance from the security force lessened. John and the leader of the Jinn reapers said we should start our hunt for the queen at the first level. Then as we cleared each group, we planted explosives. Once we were done and back in the sunlight, the mine would be destroyed. Before we could get to that point, we had to find out everything we could. I was hoping the queen would be here so we could kill her and be done with it. Instead, what we found was lab after lab. Every level was full of labs. The equipment alone must have cost hundreds of millions of dollars. It seemed to me we were down in the mine for the entire day before we reached the bottom level. When we reached this level, our teams found a group of people. They were cowering in a corner of the last lab, all of these people wore white lab coats.

"What the hell is going on here? Who the fuck are you people?" John shouted at the scientists. A smaller bespectacled man stepped forward. He tried to speak, then cleared his throat.

"We are scientists, my name is Greg Betts, and I am a virologist. Each of these people is being held captive here." The small man told John.

"Well, what the hell is going on?" I asked

"We were forced to make a disease, a new disease; it's a terrible thing. That monster had pictures of our families. She even had a video of our children sleeping in their beds." Betts told us as a tear rolled from under his glasses.

"What does it do?" Kaia asked as she and her team walked into the lab.

"It is a chimera. I was to create a virus to piggyback on a bacterium. The bacterium is a flesh-eating spoor, once the bacteria starts its job, it will die in ten hours. The medical professional will think his or her course has worked. This is when the virus wakes and starts to ravish the poor soul." The scientist told us as the others behind him nodded.

"Where is this stuff?" John asked as Kaia walked over to me.

"She has it all, the men she left behind were supposed to kill us and then meet her in the US someplace." Another scientist said.

"We took a chance and built a defect into the virus's DNA. It will only be viable for 48 hours after the bacterium dies." Another scientist added.

"What the hell are we talking about in numbers of casualties," I asked, then watched as the scientists looked at each other. John, Kaia and I could tell none of the people we found wanted to voice the dreaded number.

"It's that high, is it?" John asked, looking at the scientists before us.

"What we made has never existed before, no one has ever seen this, and when it is gone, it will never be seen again. Just like our civilization, our cultures, the human race will be halved, at least, if you don't stop her.

"She has the means to aerosol the chimera into the jet stream. There are to be three planes flying in different areas of the world. They are going to release the chimera at the same time." Another of the scientists said as she stepped forward.

"Can you tell which plane the queen is on or where she will deploy the weapon?" The Jinn leader asked. We all could hear the urgency in his voice. Within minutes we had the longitude and latitude of each deployment plane. John and the leaders of the units from different countries were in contact with military leaders. For some men and women, it was a hard pill to swallow. They had only acted with orders from the elected officials before. Each knew there was no time for debate.

We left the mine a smoking hole in the ground. The scientists were all out and leaving the mine in vehicles. All of them were frantic to get home to their families. I feared they would find only death waiting to greet them. As our custom citation x raced through the sky, none of us on the plane said a word. Then a chirp from the radar brought all the bowed heads up. We all looked, hoping we had found the mad creature hell-bent on murdering billions.

"Will your weapons take out that plane?" John asked.

"Yes, easily." The Jinn leader answered.

I sat in the co-pilot seat, watching the radar and calling out the distance to our target. Looking up from the radar, I could see a dot in the sky. Instantly I knew it was the plane we were hunting; turning in my seat, I called to John.

"We have her, she is less than five miles ahead, and her plane is climbing," I called back to my friend. Looking out the windscreen again, I watched as the queen's plane grew the closer we got to it. I could hear Kaia helping John. He would have to lie in a specially designed box we called the coffin. Jack had designed it after we had shot down my mother's plane in Patagonia. It was Jack and John who thought we might have to do it again from a higher altitude. All I could think of was how it was a shame Jack wasn't here to see it in action. I still couldn't understand how we were catching the other plane so quickly. Then as we started to pull alongside, I understood a fine vapour was issuing from canisters under the plane. As I looked into one of the portholes on the plane, I found the face of the queen smiling at me. She became confused when I smiled back and waved at her. I watched as she started to scream at someone in her plane. Then a brilliant flash caused me to flinch.

John had fired one of the weapons the Jinn carried. The team leader had worked on the weapon and had increased its power fivefold. The destruction of the other plane was catastrophic. The energy pulse hit the plane's undercarriage. The fuel was ignited, then an intense blast from the fuel and the energy pulse hit our plane. For several moments our pilot fought to regain control as we plummeted from the sky. I watched the earth racing up to meet our spinning plane. Then as if by magic, we stopped spinning, and the world settled below our wings. It was then I realized we had been too late. The queen was able to deploy some of her chimeras.

"I think we were too late," I called back to the others, my heart clenched in fear. Landing in France, our group was struck at how completely our mission had failed. Reports of a new plague to befall humanity started to come in. The leader of the Jinn contacted the leaders of his world. They offered sanctuary to all who wanted it, and many people went to the other side. We were happy to hear the elders on the other side would not accept families who had sacrificed for the queen. I begged John and Lisa to go to the other side after Jack had died from the chimera; they just smiled and hugged me.

A few months later, I wept as I placed Kaia on a pyre. She was the love of my life. On her last night on earth, she asked me to carry her out so we could see the stars together one last time. As I held her in my arms, my tears fell on her face; she never felt them. As I stood looking into the heavens with my love held in my arms, Kaia died. I stood looking up into the heavens, telling Kaia how beautiful the sky was. John and Lisa watched me for some time, then came to help me back to the house. It wasn't long after Kaia left me I had to build two more pyres for my friends. John told me on his last day that he had a son. When I looked confused he smiled and patted my face.

"It was you, Rod. You are my son; through love, you are my boy, you always have been." Those were his last words on this earth.

I held Lisa in my arms as she wept for her mother and father. We built pyres for them and stood as Lisa spoke of them. I did the same for my oldest and dearest friend when the chimera took her from me. I looked around at all the destruction, at all the death. I needed to get away from it all. I knew of a small temple on the Canadian island of Newfoundland. It was unmanned and had been for many years before the downfall of man. With society in shambles getting from France to Newfoundland took some time. There were no airlines, and the only thing to cross the night sky man-made was the international space station. Its crew was forced to watch as the world's great cities went dark one by one. The lights we took for granted to always be there dimmed then failed. As the people who worked at the plants became sick, then died, no one was left to keep the machinery running.

One year after the queen and the sick bastards who followed her released the chimera, the virus died. The world was left in the dark, and the crew on the international space station watched. Every day they would try to send a message to earth. Every day that message went unanswered. As I stood at the gates of the temple in France, I watched the station cross the night sky. I knew the people in that station had died; they would have starved to death or worse. I locked the doors of the temple, then the gates as I left the last home I knew.

Walking across the island of Newfoundland, I would stop to see if the uncountable small fishing villages held life. In some, I found people, though, like the rest of the world, they had suffered great loss. Though I can say in this tiny corner of a now larger world, they would still smile and greet me. One day I stopped and watched as a group of men buried a friend. When I asked if it had been the plague that took their friend. One of the men told me it was heartbreak that killed their friend.

"Putting his wife and children to rest did poor Pat in lad. It wasn't the plague that took him; it was his broken heart. I held my hat in hand as they lowered their friend into the ground. Then walked off, still heading for the lone temple overlooking the small village of Leading Tickles. As I walked through the island, I found graveyards full of fresh graves, the earth still mounded up. As I walked past a small church, the priest came to the doors and looked at me.

"Where is it you are off to, son?" He asked.

"Leading tickles, father," I answered as I stopped.

"You still have a bit of a walk. Is it you have family there you hope to find?" The priest asked.

"No, father, in what's left of our world, I am completely alone," I answered. Then started to walk again as I waved to the priest. Three days later, I looked at a sign announcing the village of Leading Tickles. That afternoon I was standing on the steps of the temple, looking at the locked doors.

"What is it you want in there, lad?" An old man asked me.

"The order I belong to owns this temple; I've come to live here," I answered him.

"There is nothing in there but spirits of the past." The man said as he turned and walked away. Pulling a heavy ring with two keys on it from my backpack, I unlocked the doors to the temple and entered. I stopped in the doorway of the temple to let my eyes adjust to the darkness. The windows were all covered, and so was the furniture. I never uncovered the windows. I did uncover the furniture so I could sit. That night I ate the last of my food and placed pictures of the only family I ever knew around me. Lisa and Jack held hands, both laughing.

John sitting with his favourite coffee cup, smiling at the camera and Kaia. Her long black hair was blown by the wind, her smile calling to me.

I can feel the tears on my face; as I look at my friends and family, I know they are dead because of me. Because I ran, I should have just died, so many dead. Four and a half billion men, women and children are gone, ripped from this world because I hated my mother and father.

I have written this story hoping someone will find it and tell it to others. I don't want forgiveness, I can not forgive myself. I kept one gift John gave me years before. It was his father's browning .45cal model 1911.

Holding this gift, I turn it. I can see the barrel's diameter; as I weep for my family and the billions lost, I slowly squeeze the trigger.....

The End

THE JINN

Todd LeRoux

Don't miss out!

Visit the website below and you can sign up to receive emails whenever Todd LeRoux publishes a new book. There's no charge and no obligation.

https://books2read.com/r/B-A-MMEEB-OHAYC

BOOKS2READ

Connecting independent readers to independent writers.

Did you love *The Jinn*? Then you should read *The Wanderer*[1] by Todd LeRoux!

[2]

Michael was known as the boy waiting to die in his hometown. No one ever said this to him, but everyone knew about his brain tumor, and they waited for the sad day to come. What no one, including Michael, knew was when he was injured in the car accident that killed his parents, the tumor changed to save his life. Now the tumor is changing again...one night, Michael learns how the tumor takes Micael's mind from his bed to a house where a killer is stalking a family. Michael is ripped from the nightmare of seeing a family killed by a madman. His grandparents race to his room when they hear their grandson screaming in the middle of the night. Weeks later, after another nightmare, Michael is taken to his Doctor. It was during this

---

1. https://books2read.com/u/38OqM6

2. https://books2read.com/u/38OqM6

visit Michael and his grandparents learned the tumor had changed that it was now invading deeper regions of Michael's brain with thin tendrils. On the way home, Michael sees a road sign from his dreams. Wanting to show his grandson that it was just a bad dream, Michael's grandfather turns onto the road and drives to a farm. It was this one act of a loving grandfather that started a life of running from a mad cabal of billionaires who believe they have the right to rule over the world's people.

Read more at https://www.toddleroux.com/.

Also by Todd LeRoux

The Jinn
The Wanderer
The Quest
The Island

Watch for more at https://www.toddleroux.com/.

About the Author

Todd lives on the banks of the Miramichi river. After years of working away, he now enjoys his time at home with family and friends.

Read more at https://www.toddleroux.com/.